Destined Love

Shalini Jayara

pencil

ISBN 978-93-5458-993-5
© Shalini Jayara 2021
Published in India 2021 by Pencil

A brand of
One Point Six Technologies Pvt. Ltd.
123, Building J2, Shram Seva Premises,
Wadala Truck Terminal, Wadala (E)
Mumbai 400037, Maharashtra, INDIA
E connect@thepencilapp.com
W www.thepencilapp.com

All rights reserved worldwide

No part of this publication may be reproduced, stored in or introduced into a retrieval system, or transmitted, in any form, or by any means (electronic, mechanical, photocopying, recording or otherwise), without the prior written permission of the Publisher. Any person who commits an unauthorized act in relation to this publication can be liable to criminal prosecution and civil claims for damages.

DISCLAIMER: *The opinions expressed in this book are those of the authors and do not purport to reflect the views of the Publisher.*

Author biography

A college going student, and , a writer by passion , who loves to read and write.

CONTENTS

Acknowledgements

I would like to give a big thanks to all my friends who supported me throughout , to encourage me to write , my parents and especially my sister, Sapna. But a special and big thanks to all the readers, who are investing their precious time and money in reading this story. Thank you alot.

Section1

"Hello aunty , how are you? Is Rahul awake?? " "Hello Sameera , I am good . Nope , you know how he is . He is still sleeping. " " Okay aunty , I'll go and wake him up in my style. " Sameera enters Rahul's room and throws a jug of water on him , to which he wakes up suddenly babbling. " What the hell Sameera?? You could have woke me up simply by calling my name. " said Rahul as he was babbling. " As if you would wake up then " , said Sameera while laughing. " Come on get up , we are already late for the college. It's almost a year , since, we are going to college and everyday , I have to come and wake you up , can't you get up on your own " ,said Sameera in an authoritative tone. " As if going to college regularly on time makes you a topper, you even don't know what our subjects are ", replied Rahul sarcastically while going to bathroom. After five minutes Rahul came out , dressed for the college and sat on the dining table and was having breakfast very calmly. " Eat fast, we are getting late," commanded Sameera. Rahul was still eating calmly, after he finished eating he got up and waved bye to his mom and went with Sameera on his two wheeler.

Section 2

On the way , like regularly , they were chit chatting , having fun with people walking on the roadside. Sameera and Rahul , were best friends since childhood , and ,have gone to same school and now same College. Because of them , even their families have become friends. Sameera and Rahul reached college and went towards their class. Everyone in the college were envious of their friendship. Rahul was a smart looking boy , with a sharp mind , but a bit silent because of which , all the girls were jealous of Sameera , as she was the only girl , with whom Rahul use to hang out. On the other side , Sameera was a lively girl , who use to talk to everyone around her. While the class was going on , Sameera passed a chit to Rahul in which she wrote , " we are bunking the next class." Rahul looked Sameera , and nodded his head in a No. Sameera showed him her big eyes , the teacher saw that . She immediately understood something was cooking between these two. "Why don't you go out of the classroom and complete your discussion " , said the teacher . "Get out of my class " . Sameera , happily went out and Rahul followed her. " Happy now?? We missed this period also " . Said Rahul in a angry tone . " Yess... Very happy , let's go for a movie ", said Sameera as she started walking towards the parking. With these small - small mischiefs their college days were going on , until , it was the day when they were getting graduated. Everyone was happy , finally the college was over. They were having their graduation ceremony . Rahul topped the college , as usual , and , got scholarship for a university in Banglore , for his higher studies.

Section 3

After the graduation ceremony , he asked Sameera , if she could also take admission in the same University , so that they can be together in Banglore. Sameera was silent for a moment , Rahul was very nervous , about what would be her reply. To which Sameera responded , "let's go home ". Rahul was abit upset , and , went home with her. On seeing his upset face his mother asked " what's the matter?? Why are you so upset?? " He replied , " nothing , everything is fine ", and then he headed towards his room . In his room , he was still thinking , what Sameera would reply. He became very anxious. He was tossing in the bed and finally after a while , he slept. Whereas in Sameera 's home , she was trying very hard to convince her parents. Her father initially refused boldly . " We have so many colleges here also , why is that you want to go to Bangalore only . What is so special in that college?? " asked Sameera's father. Sameera had no answer for this question , but she was determined to go to the same College , where Rahul was going. " I want to go to that college , or else I'll not study further " said Sameera angrily , and , left the room . Her father looked towards her mother , and , they both had a discussion about that. After seeing Sameera upset face , and how determined she was to go ,he said yes and moreover , he was a bit less worried , because he had alot of faith on Rahul . Sameera's mother , was also very happy on seeing , the happiness on her daughter's face.

Section 4

Next day , both of them have planned to watch a movie together . During the interval , Rahul asked Sameera again about the university. Sameera replied , with a no . Upon hearing which , Rahul felt as if someone has broken all his dreams. On seeing how upset Rahul was , Sameera started laughing immediately , and told him that she was joking and that she has convinced her parents , and she will be going along with him to Bangalore , in the same University. Both of them were very happy. After movie , they went for the dinner and then , they left for their homes. Both , of them have started their packing , and were very excited to leave . Happiness could be seen clearly on their faces .

Section 5

After two months , both Sameera and Rahul were ready to leave , standing in the airport with their parents , who came to drop them. Both of them were very excited . New city , new house , new college and the best thing , they both were together. They arranged all the things , in their new rented apartment . On the first day , when they entered the college , they were just looking at the big building of their college , students coming and going out of the college . They were really happy with their college . After the college , they went to explore Bangalore , happily wandering around the streets , eating street food and exploring new places. They would frequently come to their homes , on festivals and would spend time with their families. Everything was going very good , and both of them have completed their studies in the university. On Sameera's twenty third birthday , Rahul had arranged a surprise for her . He took her with him , and when Sameera saw the surprise , she was very happy . Rahul nervously went on his knees , and , proposed her , to which Sameera excitedly said yes. Rahul was on top of the seven skies. One year passed by , and finally they told their families that they want to get married. Their families raised no objections , as they knew both of them , from a long time.

Section 6

The wedding day came , Sameera was getting ready in one of the rooms , in the venue. Her face was blooming like a flower. Her parents were very happy. Their was music playing all around . The guests have arrived , even Rahul's parents have arrived ,and , everyone was waiting for Rahul , but he didn't arrived. Hours passed by , Sameera felt like , ages have passed but there was no sign of Rahul coming. She felt like thousands of arrows piercing her heart. She called Rahul , " Rahul where are you?? Everyone is waiting for you , please come fast " to which Rahul responded he is on his way and is coming , and then he hung up the phone . Sameera was a bit relieved and told everyone , that he is on his way ,and , he will be here anytime . Everyone was waiting patiently , one hour passed and there was no sign of Rahul . Rahul's parents , Sameera's parents , and , even guests were getting impatient . But , more than these people , Sameera was the one whose eyes were fixed at the entrance , she felt like time has stopped , and the destiny doesn't want Rahul to reach .

Section 7

After waiting so long , guests started leaving . Rahul's parents apologized to sameera's parents and Sameera , and left with their heads down. Sameera's parents felt insulted , and more than that , they were disheartened to see Sameera's condition . Sameera was crying in her room , throwing things here and there. That same night , Rahul called Sameera many times , but ,she didn't picked his call and in frustration blocked him. He tried his best to contact her , went her home , but he could not get through her. Sameera was in a very bad condition . She would not go out of her room , not talking to anyone , and would not eat . On seeing their daughter's condition like this , her parents , decided to do something . After two weeks , Sameera and her family shifted Paris , where her parents decided to get her married to Sameera's dad's friend son named Saurabh . She didn't wanted to , but then she thought that earlier , her parents , for her happiness , agreed to get her married to Rahul , and she was betrayed . So , this time , for her parents' happiness , she respected her parents decision , and decided to get married . She wanted to tell Saurabh everything , but her parents told her not to. Still , somehow she told him everything .

Section 8

Saurabh seemed to be a great guy , very sorted and Sameera's past didn't bother him . Sameera soon got married to Saurabh . Rahul got to know about her marriage through their common friends. After hearing this , he felt like not living anymore. He somehow managed his emotions , and started focusing on his work. He would remain busy with his work , would spend entire day , and sometimes nights in the office only . His mother , was very concerned for him . By looking at his condition , she decided to get him married . " No , I don't want to get married , I am happy as I am " said Rahul in a frustrating tone. " So you wish to remain unmarried throughout your life , for someone who didn't bother to listen to you , and without even thinking about you , got married also. " replied Rahul's mother and left his room with an upset face. On seeing his parents streesed for himself , he finally decided to get married. His mother was dancing with Joy. Within two years Rahul got married .

Section 9

After twenty years ,

"Mumma , I want to go New York for a trip . Please let me go . Papa , please convince mumma to let me go. " " No means no , Ridhi " scolded Sameera to her daughter. "But mumma , I am no more a kid . I want to go , all my friends are going , "said Ridhi while walking towards her room and banged her door. "Let her go. Even if you will not allow , she may go without your permission " said Saurabh to Sameera. Sameera has never sent Ridhi sa far from herself . But this time , TRidhi was very determined to go . Thinking very hard about it , Sameera finally agreed , and then , Ridhi was busy , shopping and packing with her friends .

Within a week , Ridhi left with her friends for New York . Ridhi was very happy , as she always wanted to see New York and explore it , and moreover , this was the first time , she has come so far from her home alone . Ridhi and her friends , booked their beds in a hostel ,where some students ,were already their. They interacted with each other , and soon became friends.

Section10

Next morning ,Ridhi and her friends were going for outing , when she thought of asking Sonu , who was also a guest in the hostel , to join them with her friends , as they could hang out together. Sonu happily said yes , and all of them went together. Everyday , they all would go together , and hang out together. Ridhi and Sonu , both were so happy together , that when their happiness started turning into feeling for each other , they even didn't know. Firstly , they were not ready , to accept the fact that they had feelings for each other , and , they started avoiding each other. Thinking about many things , like their families , the society , and all those people , who will mock them , after knowing all this . They thought , avoiding each other would help them , but it didn't . Instead they started feeling distressed . They finally understood , that they were not wrong , and happily accepted to face all the obstacles , coming infront of them. After few days , it was time for Sonu to leave for her home. Ridhi was very sad . On seeing that , Sonu asked Ridhi to come with her to her home and meet her dad , the only member in her family , as her mother died , when she was very young. Ridhi pondered for a moment , and happily agreed. That same night , Ridhi decided to call her parents ,and tell them about everything . Ridhi told them , that she met a girl , name Sonu , and they both love each other. On hearing this , her mother and father were shocked , but her father quickly changed his expression , and was showing being cool with this . He told her , he was happy for her , so he took the responsibility , of convincing her mother , who has just left the room in an upset mood . Infront of Ridhi , Saurabh was very happy for his daughter , and , told her that they will come to New York soon , and meet Sonu and her dad.

Section11

When Sonu went home , her father was very happy to see her , they both hugged each other. Then Sonu's father saw Ridhi , to which Sonu responded that she is her friend , and have come to stay with them for a few days. Sonu's father smiled at Ridhi , and told both of them to come inside . On the other hand , in Paris , Saurabh was trying his best to convince Sameera , that she needs to think about their daughter's happiness . Sameera was still silent , Saurabh lost all his hopes , and he left the room . Sameera could not sleep the whole night . Thinking about Ridhi , and then she was still in a dilemma , about what to do. She turned off the lights of her room , and again sat down , thinking about something.

Section12

Whereas , at Sonu's house , at night , after dinner , Sonu went to her father's room , she was hesitating a bit . Seeing her hestitation , her dad comforted her , and said , " no matter what I will always stand by you " . Upon hearing this , Sonu gathered some confidence , and told him everything , about Ridhi and herself. On hearing this , Sonu's father was silent for a moment. Sonu got very scared , thinking what her father will say. Her father told her , to go to her room and sleep . Sonu went out of her father's room , and went to Ridhi's room. Ridhi asked Sonu what her father said , to which Sonu replied ," he was silent " . Both of them were scared , they could not sleep whole night . Next morning , Sonu and Ridhi were having breakfast , when suddenly Sonu's father came . On seeing him , both of them stood from their seats and remained silent . Suddenly he spoke , both of them looked towards him nervously. " Ridhi when are your parents coming to New York . I want to meet them , and talk about both of you. " On hearing this both of them became very happy and were dancing with joy. Sonu hugged her father happily.

Section 13

After few days , Saurabh somehow convinced Sameera , to go and meet them. Sameera and Saurabh came to New York , and went to Sonu's house to meet her dad. Ridhi and Sonu , were very excited they were feeling at top of the world. Ridhi went to escort her parents at the gate . Hello mom , hello dad , "I am very happy to see you " by saying this she hugged them and took them inside. Sameera was not very happy , she was still making up her mind for all this . Inside the living room , Sonu was sitting on the sofa waiting for them. On their arrival , she got up , " Hello uncle , Hello aunty , nice to see you. Please have a seat. Dad is coming in a while. " Sameera and Saurabh nooded , and sat down. Few moments later , Sonu's father arrived and Sameera got up from her seat . " Rahul you are Sonu's dad??" asked Sameera shockingly. "Sameera , you! Hi , it's been so long. How have you been? Nice to see you after so many years. " Everyone was looking at both of them. Upon hearing the name Rahul , Saurabh broke the glass which he was holding . Everyone panciked . " I am fine it's nothing" said Saurabh. "You both know each other ? " asked Ridhi and Sonu. To which Sameera responded " yes we were childhood friends. " On hearing this , Rahul was a bit sad. He told Sameera to take a seat , and sat opposite to her. All the three adults chatted . Sameera was still making her mind , when suddenly , Saurabh agreed , for Ridhi and

Sonu's marriage. Finally , all the three , decided that they will get both of their daughters married. Then Sameera and Saurabh got up to leave , and told Ridhi to come with them. Three of them left. At the hotel room , when Sameera told her father about all this , how Ridhi wants to get married to a girl , that too Rahul's daughter , Sameera's father clearly refused. He told her , that this is not acceptable by him and the society , and he no longer trusts Rahul. Sameera tried to convince her father alot , that they should be concerned about their daughter's happiness , not what the society thinks , and , as far as Rahul is concerned , she herself has not forgotten what he has done to her. But , she decided to keep her daughter's happiness first. But , still Sameera's father was not convinced. Sameera decided , that no matter what , she will get her daughter married.

Section 14

After one year. In one of the most popular five star hotel of Paris , Ridhi and Sonu were getting married. Everything was set . But this time of one year , was not easy for both the families . Both the families, were getting threatening letters , indicating them , that they will not let this marriage take place , and it was better that , they call off the marriage by themselves . But still , both the families were determined to conduct the marriage . Sameera was abit worried , for both the kids . She knew that , the culprit was amongst they know . As , the discussion about marriage , was not known to many people . She suspected everyone around her . She got the handwriting , in the letters examined . She got to know , whose handwriting it was . After seeing the results , she was shocked . Still she remained silent , thinking , till the time the kids are safe , she'll not confront the culprit . All this , was happening for one year . Finally , at the day of the marriage .

Section 15

Ridhi was there at the venue. All the guests have arrived, Sameera and Saurabh were there , Rahul was there and , everyone was waiting for Sonu. An hour passed by , but Sonu did not arrived. Everyone started gossiping. Ridhi was staring at the gate , waiting for Sonu . Sameera became nostalgic , by thinking , how the same situation took place , when Rahul did not arrived on their wedding day and , how she was shattered. She did not wanted her daughter , to go through the same pain. She was scared , what if , just like Rahul , Sonu also did not arrive . She was immersed in these thoughts , when her father came to her side and told her , " see I told you not to trust Rahul. What the father did his daughter is doing the same. " Sameera came out of her thoughts. She was very worried , and , saw Rahul. Sameera started walking towards Rahul . " Where the hell is Sonu?? Is she going to come , or just like you didn't arrived at that time she will also not arrive this time ? "

Section 16

Sameera was so worried , and then , looking at her daughter , who was loosing all her hope and breaking down. She could not control her emotions. She regretted trusting Rahul and Sonu. All sorts of bad thoughts, were coming in her mind. She was continuously asking Rahul about Sonu , " where is she??? How can she do this?? Speak up Rahul , where is Sonu??"

Section 17

Rahul was about to say something , when suddenly , Sonu arrived. She apologized to everyone and told " I was on my way , when suddenly , Ridhi's message came , that she wanted to meet me before the marriage . I arrived at the place , but she was not there , and someone hitted me . I somehow sat in my car , and reached here ."

Section 18

There was an awkward silence , after what Sonu said. Sameera's father , was laughing mockingly , "you think , we are going to trust you , on all this. ?? Do we look like fools to you?? ". " No uncle , I am telling you the truth. If you don't believe me you can ask the doctor, from whom I have got my dressing done." replied Sonu. Sameera's father was just finding ways , how he can call off the marriage.

Section 19

After hearing this , everyone was shocked and worried . Ridhi came forward and said , " I didn't message you . Infact , my phone was not with me . It was with dad. How is all this possible ? " There was absolute silence .

Section 20

Everyone started running their minds , thinking is Sonu telling the truth ? If yes , who would have done this?? Thinking how Sameera's father , was wanting to call off the wedding, maybe he was the one behind all this. Rahul , was also looking towards Sameera's father. But she said , her phone was with her dad, so who could message Sonu from Ridhi's phone??

Section 21

There were alot of questions, in everyone's mind. But what was more shocking , that Sameera , was standing silently in one corner . She was immersed into deep thoughts . Everyone was scared , thinking what was going in her mind. Everyone present there, were arguing , blaming each other, giving justification .

Section 22

When , there came a voice of a slap . Sameera had slapped Saurabh . Everyone present there was puzzled . " What the hell Sameera . Why did you slap me ?? questioned Saurabh in anger . " You want to know why ?? Why did you message Sonu from Ridhi's phone ?" Questioned Sameera in an authoritative tone . " No mom , what are you saying ??why would dad do it ?? He was the one , to convince you . He is really happy for me . " " Sonu , Ridhi , you remember those threatening letters ?? I got them examined. The person , who wrote them , was Saurabh . I chose to remain silent , thinking , till the time no one is harmed , I'll not confront him . But today he has crossed, all his limits ."

Section 23

Sonu was shocked , she started questioning her dad, " why dad , why , why would you do that. You have always supported me , I thought you understand my love . You also love mom , how would you feel , if someone would do something like this , to mom and you. I thought , nanu don't understand my love , but you proved me wrong.. It was you who don't understand true love. You are the one , because of which I could have lost my love today , you broke my trust . I will never trust you again. "

Section 24

Out of anger , Saurabh burst out , " yes ,yes , I did all this , because everyone I loved , never loved me back equally . Back then , my parents also loved my elder sister more than me , so I killed her . Sameera also , never loved me . So, how could I let my daughter , get married to someone's daughter , who was the first love , of my wife . If I could not get the love I wanted , then no one can .So I did all this . " Everyone was shocked , Ridhi broke down. Sonu consoled her . Rahul called the cops , and Saurabh got arrested .

Section 25

After some time ,

The wedding rituals started taking place. Sameera and Rahul ,were standing together. By seeing Sonu and Ridhi , getting married , they became nostalgic. How they both loved each other so much , and , were so happy on their weeding day. Suddenly , a drop of tear flowed from Sameera's eye , and , Rahul saw that. He offered his hankerchief to her . Sameera did not take it , and , finally spoke out , " why Rahul , why didn't you came on the weeding day ?" Rahul was very calm , he responded "I was coming Sameera but as I was on my way , I was abducted by some goons , and , they took me somewhere. They misunderstood me, by someone else and even took away my cellphone and everything. When they realised , I was not the one they were supposed to pick up , they left me all alone to that mysterious place . I was left with no phone , no money. How could I have contacted you?? " On hearing this , Sameera was shocked , and , was very angry on herself. She realised it was her mistake. Had she heard him once , then the situation would be something else. To which Rahul said, " what's gone is gone . Our story was left incomplete , maybe because Ridhi and Sonu's story was destined to be completed. " Sameera smiled at Rahul. Both of them ,were very happy for their daughters. On that day , everyone was very happy. Sameera's father got proved wrong . Sonu and Ridhi , were now a happily married couple. Sameera's misunderstandings were clear now. Rahul and sameera , were now best friends again.

www.ingramcontent.com/pod-product-compliance
Lightning Source LLC
LaVergne TN
LVHW050428160726
843469LV00041B/1278